For Sreeya, Harry, and Thomas
~S.P.

To my Jon, for untying all
my knots and tangles
~M.P.

The art in this book was created digitally.

Cataloging-in-Publication Data has been applied for and may be obtained from the Library of Congress.

ISBN 978-1-4197-6158-4

Text © 2021 Sandhya Parappukkaran
Illustrations © 2021 Michelle Pereira
Book design by Pooja Desai and Jade Rector

Printed and bound in China
10 9 8 7 6 5 4 3 2 1

ABRAMS The Art of Books
195 Broadway, New York, NY 10007
abramsbooks.com

THE BOY WHO TRIED TO SHRINK HIS NAME

By
Sandhya Parappukkaran

Illustrated by
Michelle Pereira

Abrams Books for Young Readers 🌸 New York

My name is Zimdalamashkermishkada.

It trips me up every morning, like
long shoelaces that always come undone.

It's my first day at a new school,
and I need a shorter name.

One I can throw in the air
and catch with a single hand.

I shrink my name in the dryer on a superhot double cycle before the bus arrives.

POOF!

My name springs back to life like a scared puffer fish at sea.

In class, Miss Clarity fills the board with math problems. "Buddy up!" she says.

I crumple my name into a tight ball and turn to Elly.

She writes down her name, then asks me how to spell mine.

BANG!

My name explodes like
a crack of thunder.

After recess, Miss Clarity
calls for line leaders.

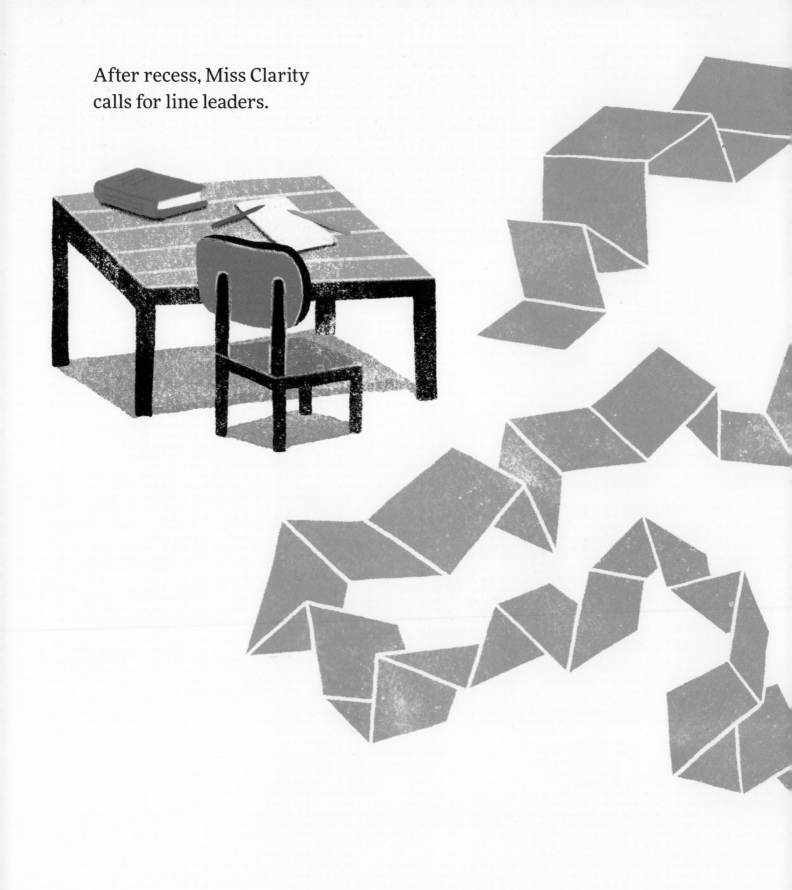

I fold my name horizontally, then vertically
a million times before raising my hand.

Miss Clarity smiles.
"Can you say your name again?"

It unfolds to its original size,
like origami in reverse.

When the last bell rings, I push past the laughter, squish through the sideways glances, and bump into Elly at the gate.

"Yes," I say firmly, finally shrinking my name. "My name is Zim."

As soon as I get home, I ask Mom if I can change my name to "Zim." Her eyes move from the swirling curry to mine.

"We named you after the coconut trees that stretch high and hold up the sky while sheltering all underneath," she says. "Give people a chance to say it right."

A deep breath helps me stand up tall and grab my board.
I roll out of the house and into the park.

"Hey, Zim!" yells Elly.

My voice whispers, "It's Zimdala . . ." Then I stop.

She drops into the ramp and turns at the top.

"Wow! How did you learn that?" I ask.

"Practice." Elly shrugs.

She shows me where to step on the board to start the trick.

Copying Elly, I press my foot down but tumble into the ramp.

"Are you okay, Zim?"

"Yes. Um, it's **ZIM-DALA** ..." I start off my name.

I ride the ramp slowly, not reaching full height.
Elly shows me how to make the turn. I try, but topple over.

"**ZIM-DALA-MASH** ..."

I stretch out my name further for Elly.

Elly walks me home, and Mom
calls out for us to pick some banana leaves.

My ears turn red when Mom says my name, but
Elly is already tearing off the striped green leaves.

Every day, Elly helps me creep higher and higher.
I lift my wheels to turn, only to tumble over again.

"ZIM-DALA-MASH-KER…"

I extend my name
a little more.

At home, Mom has rice flour dough ready.
She invites Elly in. Elly's eyes widen at the
coconut snowflakes falling onto the plate.
Mom mixes the snow with crumbled palm sugar.

Elly and I go to the park every day.
Other kids from school join us. I can make the
turn now, but my landings are still wobbly.

"ZIM-DALA-MASH-KER-MISH..."

I've almost unfolded my whole name.

Back home, we spread dough over banana leaves like Mom does. Elly sprinkles sweet snow on one side. Mom closes the parcel like a book and cooks it on the heat. We sit around the table munching soft ada and sticky coconut filling.

We keep on practicing, again and again and again.
Then one day, I make the full turn!

Everyone yells and cheers.
"Go, Zim! You did it!"

Elly swoops down beside me and calls out . . .

"His name is

ZIMDALAMASHKERMISHKADA!"